ON ISRAEL'S 30th ANNIVERSARY SABRAMAN COMICS PRESENT
THE FIRST-EVER ISRAELI SUPER-HERO COMIC
NO. 1
NOVEMBER 1978
THE INCREDIBLE ADVENTURES OF ISRAEL'S MIGHTY SUPER-HERO
THE POWERS OF A SUPERMAN ...
THE COURAGE OF THE SABRA ...
THE FAITH OF ABRAHAM ...
SABRAMAN
DRAWN AND WRITTEN BY URI FINK
THRILLS!!!
ACTION!!!
EXCITEMENT!!!
1ST ISSUE
MORE THAN 200 PICTURES!!
© 1978 SABRAMAN COMICS, ISRAEL

SOMEWHERE IN THE JUDEAN DESERT THERE'S A SECRET PASSAGE THAT LEADS TO THE BASE OF
THE SUPER AGENCY OF ISRAEL

THE SUPER AGENCY PROTECTS THE COUNTRY FROM DANGERS THAT CANNOT BE HANDLED BY THE POLICE OR BY THE ARMY. ALTHOUGH THE ISRAELI AGENCY WAS VERY DEVELOPED, IT ONLY LACKED ONE THING...
SUPER HEROES!!!

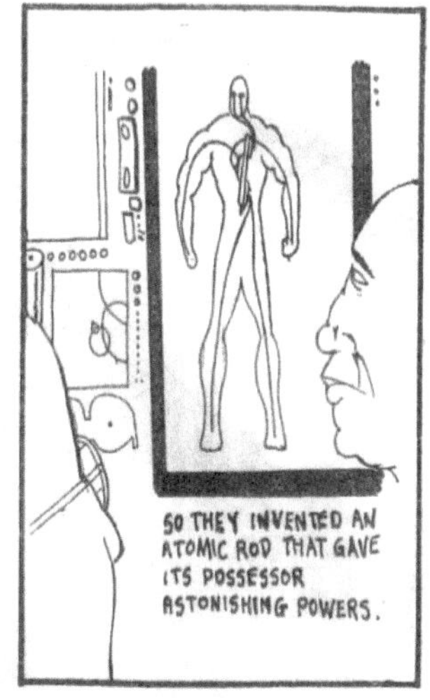
SO THEY INVENTED AN ATOMIC ROD THAT GAVE ITS POSSESSOR ASTONISHING POWERS.

BUT, AS THEY WERE ABOUT TO PLANT THE ROD IN THE 18th MAN...

...AN EXPLOSION OCCURRED.
KAB-OOM!
ISRAEL SECURITY OPERATIONS

THE RADIOACTIVE ENERGY SPREAD THROUGHOUT HIS BODY
BECAUSE OF THE LARGE AMOUNT OF ENERGY IN HIS BODY SHIN-18 CAN SHOOT RADIOACTIVE RAYS OUT OF HIS EYES.

ZAP
ZAP
ZAP
HE CAN ALSO CREATE A MAGNETIC FORCE FIELD AROUND HIS BODY WHICH IS INVULNERABLE TO ATTACK.

History of the Super Agents
YOU PROBABLY WONDER WHAT A SUPER AGENT IS? WELL, HERE ARE ALL THE ANSWERS.

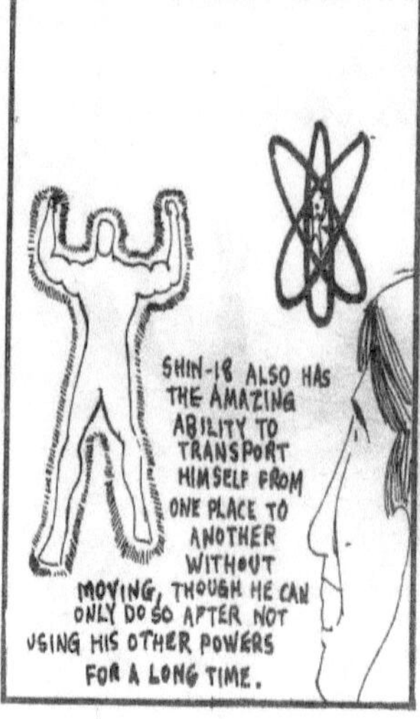
SHIN-18 ALSO HAS THE AMAZING ABILITY TO TRANSPORT HIMSELF FROM ONE PLACE TO ANOTHER WITHOUT MOVING, THOUGH HE CAN ONLY DO SO AFTER NOT USING HIS OTHER POWERS FOR A LONG TIME.

W.W.II
1942
IT ALL BEGAN DURING WORLD WAR II IN 1942...

AN AMERICAN CALLED JIM STEVENS INVENTED AN ARMOR THAT GAVE ITS WEARER INCREDIBLE STRENGTH.

SO THE FIRST AGENT WAS CREATED.

HE HAD PHENOMENAL SUCCESS...

BUT THE GERMANS CREATED THEIR OWN AGENT- NAZIMAN.

THE MOST FAMOUS BATTLE BETWEEN THE TWO SUPER-AGENTS WAS AT THE END OF THE WAR IN 1945.

THEN ALL THE OTHER COUNTRIES CREATED THEIR SUPER AGENTS.
SWEDEN
FRANCE
ICELAND
U.S.A
SPAIN

SHIN-18 IS SABRAMAN!
DAN BAR-ON, THE EX-ISRAEL ARMY CAPTAIN, IS SUPER AGENT SHIN-18, KNOWN TO THE WORLD AS SABRAMAN.

RATATATATATAT
DAN'S PARENTS WERE KILLED BY THE NAZIS IN POLAND DURING THE HOLOCAUST. AFTER THE WAR HE IMMIGRATED TO ISRAEL.

AFTER THE WAR DAN BECAME A MEMBER OF THE ISRAEL POLICE FORCE FIGHTING CRIME WHEREVER IT APPEARED.

BOOOM
HE TOOK PART IN THE SINAI CAMPAIGN AND THE SIX-DAY WAR.

KA-BOOM
IN THE YOM KIPPUR WAR DAN WAS BADLY WOUNDED.

WHILE HE WAS RECOVERING IN THE HOSPITAL, THE ISRAELI SUPER-AGENCY ASKED HIM TO BECOME ONE OF THE 20 ISRAELI SUPER-AGENTS. OF COURSE, DAN AGREED.

DAN AND HIS WIFE DINA ARE IN THEIR COTTAGE IN AFEKA ENJOYING A SOCIAL GATHERING, WHEN OUR STORY BEGINS...

SUDDENLY DAN FEELS A SHARP PAIN. PERHAPS IT IS BECAUSE OF HIS OLD WOUND... PERHAPS

DAN SPRINGS OUT OF THE ROOM INTO THE GARDEN.
HEY, DAN!

DAN TAKES OUT A STRANGE BOX.
AGENT SHIN-18, ARE YOU READY FOR THE ATOMIC TRANSFORMATION?
I'M READY, BOSS!

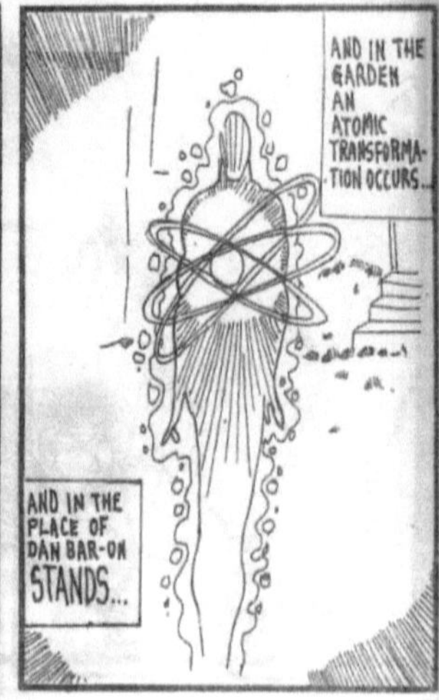
AND IN THE GARDEN AN ATOMIC TRANSFORMATION OCCURS...
AND IN THE PLACE OF DAN BAR-ON STANDS...

SUPER-AGENT SHIN-18
SABRAMAN

WITH HIS AMAZING ABILITY TO DEFY THE FORCE OF GRAVITY SABRAMAN RISES...

WITH ASTONISHING SPEED HE FLIES OVER THE JUDEAN DESERT

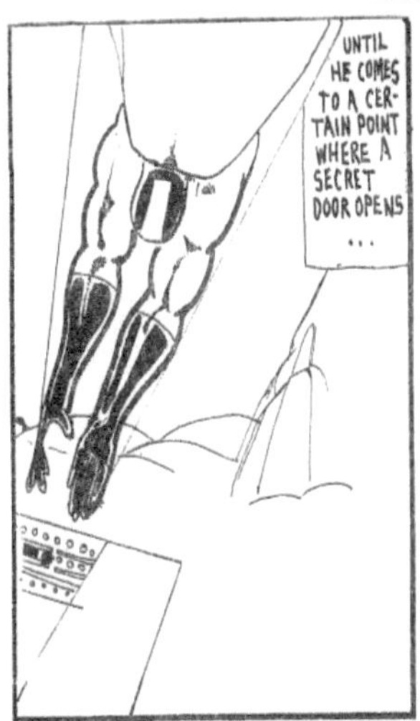
UNTIL HE COMES TO A CERTAIN POINT WHERE A SECRET DOOR OPENS ...

OKAY, BOSS, I'M HERE! WHAT DO YOU WANT ?
SABRAMAN ENTERS THE BASE.

HAVE A SEAT SABRAMAN.

WE REALLY NEED YOU THIS TIME !

YESTERDAY SOMEONE BROKE INTO A SECRET BASE. HE KILLED THE GUARD AND STOLE SOME HIGHLY SECRET CODED FILES...
OUR CAMERAS SHOW THE THIEF IS A HIRE AGENT* CALLED HYPERMAN.
*A HIRE AGENT IS A SUPER AGENT WHO HIRES HIMSELF TO THE HIGHEST BIDDER.

THIS IS HYPERMAN. HE IS IMMENSELY STRONG AND HE CAN FLY AT SUPER SPEED. HE IS A VERY DANGEROUS ADVERSARY.

THAT'S SOME STORY, BOSS! I'VE GOT TO GET THOSE FILES!
YES, I'LL GIVE YOU HIS PRESENT LOCATION.

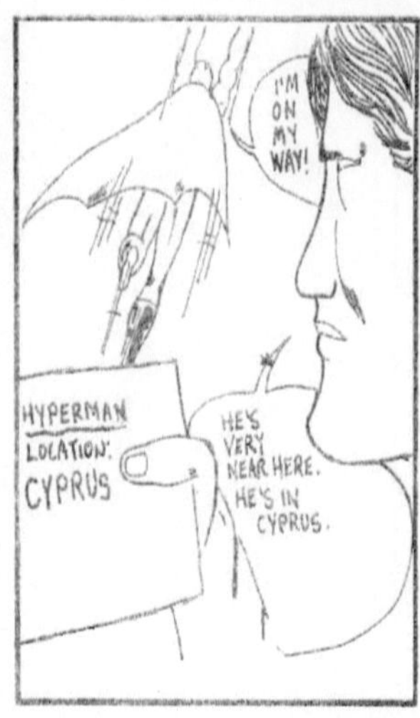
I'M ON MY WAY!
HYPERMAN
LOCATION: CYPRUS
HE'S VERY NEAR HERE. HE'S IN CYPRUS.

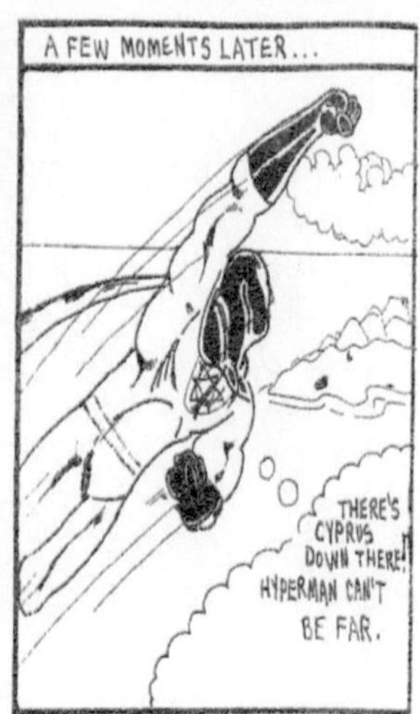
A FEW MOMENTS LATER...
THERE'S CYPRUS DOWN THERE! HYPERMAN CAN'T BE FAR.

HERE HE COMES! I HOPE HE'LL GIVE ME THE FILES PEACEFULLY...

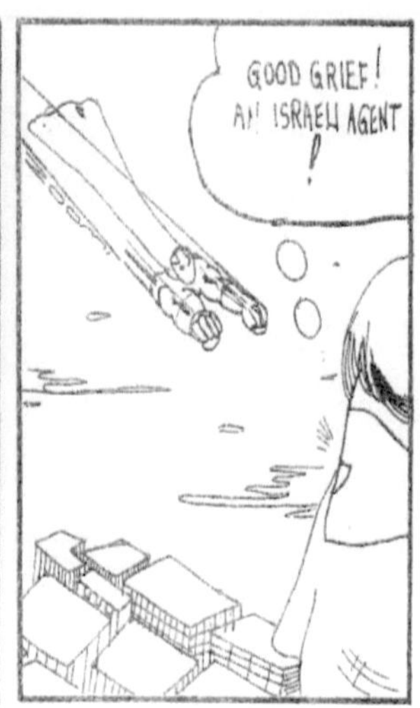
GOOD GRIEF! AN ISRAELI AGENT!

POW

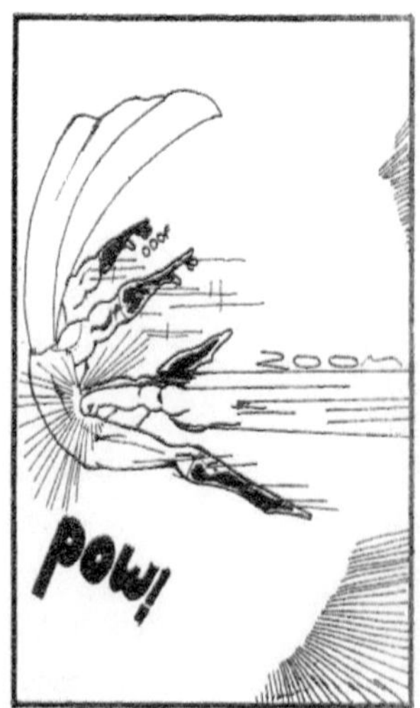
POW!

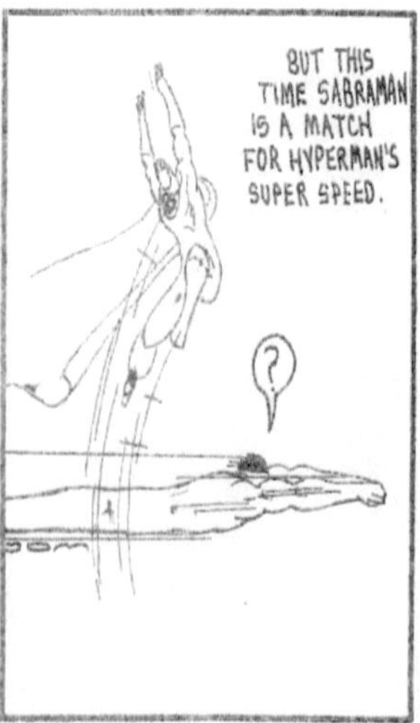
BUT THIS TIME SABRAMAN IS A MATCH FOR HYPERMAN'S SUPER SPEED.
?

HERE HE COMES AGAIN!

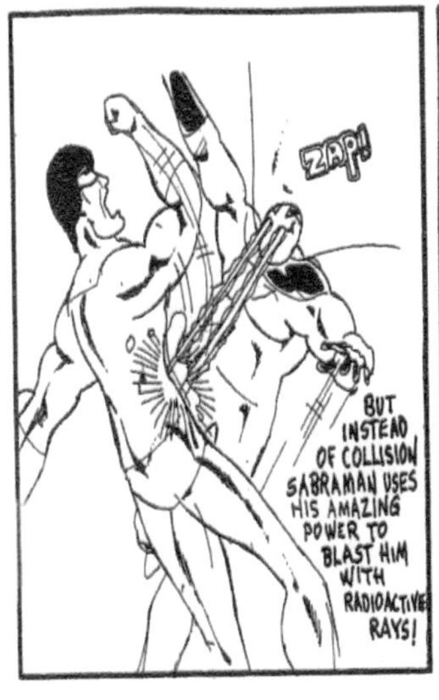
ZAP!
BUT INSTEAD OF COLLISION SABRAMAN USES HIS AMAZING POWER TO BLAST HIM WITH RADIOACTIVE RAYS!

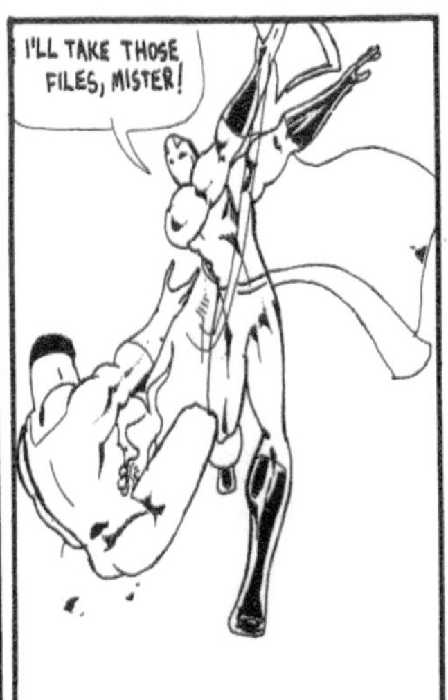
I'LL TAKE THOSE FILES, MISTER!

OH, NO. HERE HE COMES, AGAIN! SOMEONE PAID HIM A LOT FOR THE FILES. I'M CURIOUS TO KNOW WHAT'S IN THEM ...

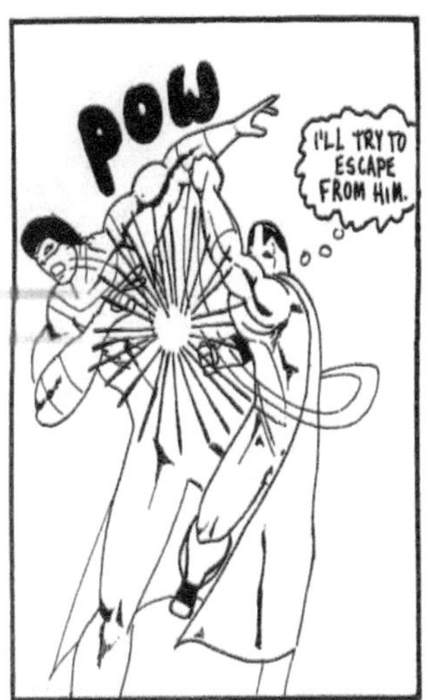
POW
I'LL TRY TO ESCAPE FROM HIM.

I GUESS HE'S TOO FAST FOR ME. IF I WANT TO GET AWAY FROM HIM I'LL HAVE TO USE ...

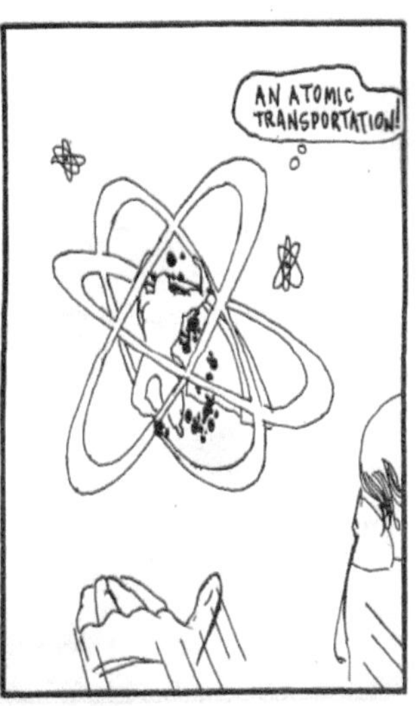
AN ATOMIC TRANSPORTATION!

LATER, BACK IN ISRAEL...
HERE ARE THE FILES, BOSS!

WOW !! JUST LISTEN TO THIS!
COMPUTER

MAN ALIVE!!! IT'S A PLAN FOR A MACHINE THAT TAKES OVER THE HUMAN MIND. NO WONDER HE WANTED IT SO MUCH.
CODE FILE ✱X222 INVASION OF THE HUMAN MIND

WELL, WHAT ARE YOU WAITING FOR? CALL FOR AN INTERNATIONAL INVESTIGATION. SOMEONE IS TRYING TO TAKE OVER THE WORLD!!
YOU KNOW VERY WELL, SABRAMAN, THERE ISN'T ENOUGH EVIDENCE TO START AN INTERNATIONAL INVESTIGATION. WE CAN'T OPERATE ON THIS CASE WITHOUT PERMISSION OF OUR SUPERIORS.

BUT...
I HAVE TO REPORT MY ACTIVITIES EVERY TWO DAYS. I'LL GIVE YOU TWO DAYS TO FIND ENOUGH PROOF TO START AN INVESTIGATION. I'LL SEND YOU AN ASSISTANT.

LATER — AS SABRAMAN FLIES OVER ISRAEL

I'M BET-5, YOUR ASSISTANT, SHALOM, SABRAMAN!
SHALOM, BET-5. I'M PLEASED TO MEET YOU!

WELL, WHEN DO WE START?
I GUESS WE'LL HAVE TO WAIT UNTIL HIS NEXT MOVE.

MEANWHILE IN A SECRET CAVE...
I'M SORRY, BOSS, BUT HE TOOK THE FILES FROM ME!
YOU FAILED, YOU CLUMSY FOOL. I'LL HAVE TO ELIMINATE YOU!

ARE YOU CRAZY? WHAT CAN AN OLD MAN LIKE YOU DO TO HYPERMAN ?!

GULP!!! ... YOU'RE NOT HUMAN! YOUR HAND.. IT'S...

BAH!
I KNEW THAT FOOL WASN'T STRONG ENOUGH FOR ME. I'VE GOT TO GET REAL HELP... THE BEST HELP...

CIA
RINNNG
CIA

YOU!! WHAT DO YOU WANT ?
HELLO STEVENS, HOW ARE THINGS AT THE CIA?

I WANT A CERTAIN ISRAELI SUPER-AGENT ELIMINATED! I WANT THE BEST MAN ON THE JOB! THE STRONGEST!! AND I WANT THE BODY. DO AS I SAY AND I WON'T TELL ANYONE ABOUT YOUR PAST.
O.O.OKAY... GET ME...

...POWERMAN!
YOU CALLED BOSS ?
THAT GUY WILL BE BROUGHT TO YOU IN A FEW MOMENTS!

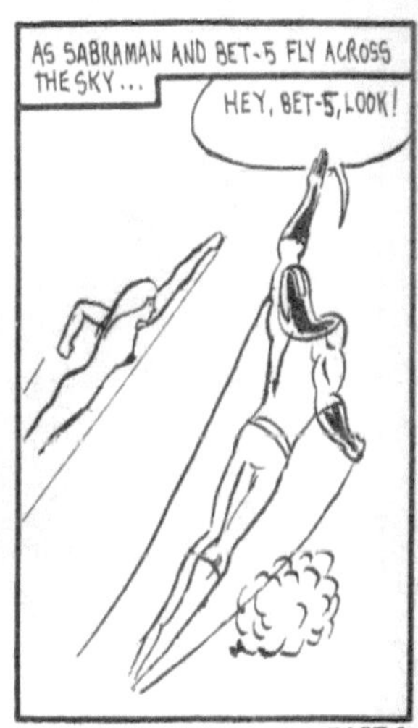
AS SABRAMAN AND BET-5 FLY ACROSS THE SKY...
HEY, BET-5, LOOK!

HEY, WHAT'S THAT ?

I'LL CATCH IT!
THE BODY OF HYPERMAN

IT'S THE CRUSHED BODY OF HYPERMAN! OUR MAN IS NOT ONLY A THIEF. HE IS A MURDERER!
GASP!!! LOOK AT HIS NECK!

THERE ARE MY TARGETS! THEY DON'T LOOK TOO STRONG FOR ME!

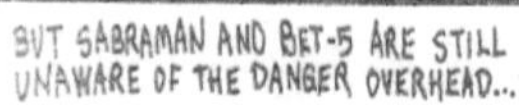
BUT SABRAMAN AND BET-5 ARE STILL UNAWARE OF THE DANGER OVERHEAD...

POWERMAN ATTACKS...

I'LL GET YOU, YOU EVIL MONSTER!

GASP!
WHAT DOES AN AMERICAN SUPER-AGENT WANT FROM ME ?
HE'S TOO STRONG FOR ME... HE'S CRUSHING ME!

SABRAMAN CONCENTRATES ALL HIS RADIOACTIVE POWER AND FINALLY...

IF THIS DOESN'T FINISH HIM, I'VE HAD IT BECAUSE I'VE USED UP ALL MY ENERGY!

BUT POWERMAN DOESN'T SEEM AT ALL IMPRESSED...
PAM!

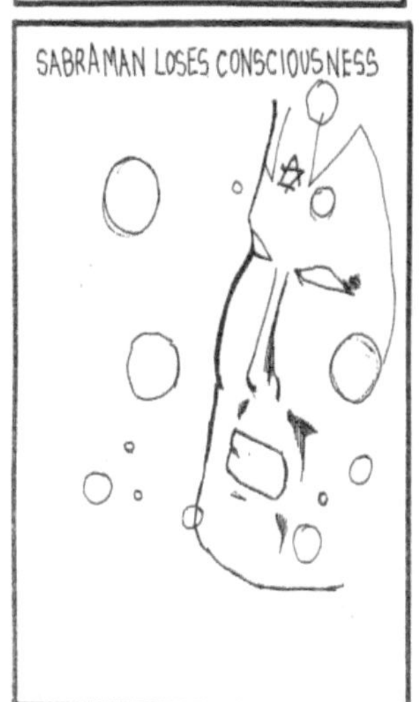
SABRAMAN LOSES CONSCIOUSNESS

SEVERAL HOURS LATER IN THE UNDER-GROUND DUNGEON...
UHHM...
WELL, WELL, MY FRIEND. AWAKE AT LAST!

IT'S NO USE TRYING TO ESCAPE, MY FRIEND, THE CHAINS EXACTLY MATCH YOUR POWER!

WHY DON'T YOU RELAX? I'LL TOUCH YOU WITH MY RADIOACTIVE HAND AND YOU'LL DIE.
HAHAHAHAHA!!!
O.K. ARE YOU READY FOR THE END?

AHA, THE LADY IS AWAKE! I'LL HANDLE HER FIRST!
UHMM...

HELLO, LITTLE GIRL. LOOK WHO'S COMING!
DON'T BE SCARED, IT'S ONLY DEATH! HA HA HAHAHAHA

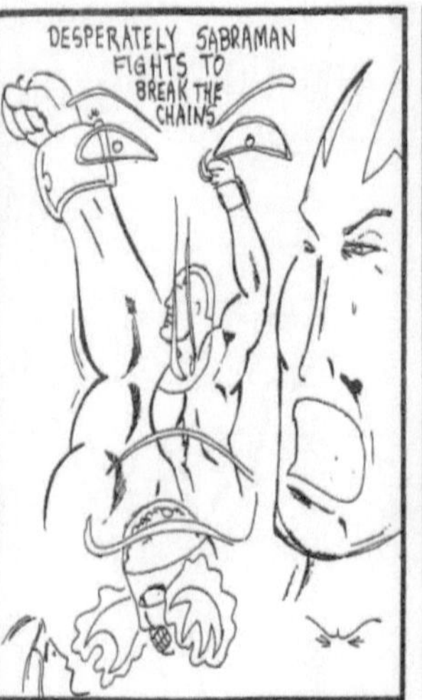
DESPERATELY SABRAMAN FIGHTS TO BREAK THE CHAINS

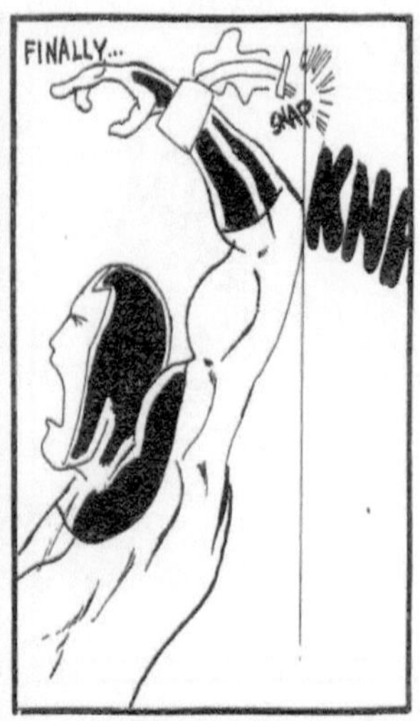
FINALLY...
SNAP
KNA

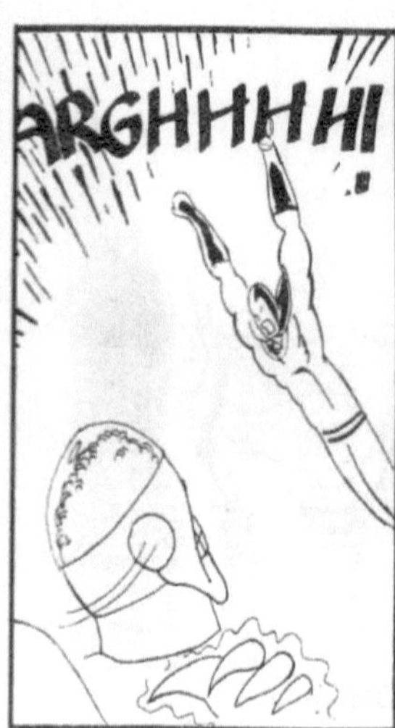
ARGHHHH!

POW!

LOOK OUT!
SUDDENLY, DEADLY RADIATION STREAMS OUT OF THE CEILING.

QUICK! WE'RE BOTH POOPED, AND YOU'RE HIT, BET-5.
LET'S GET OUT OF HERE!!

LATER, AT HASHOMER HOSPITAL NEAR TEL AVIV... BET-5 LIES FIGHTING FOR HER LIFE.
I'LL GET YOU FOR THIS, WHOEVER YOU ARE. I SWEAR!

ONCE AGAIN SABRAMAN BECOMES DAN BAR-ON...
I CAN'T HELP FEELING RESPONSIBLE FOR THE GIRL.

SUDDENLY DAN HEARS A STRANGE VOICE FROM THE SKY...
IF YOU WANT TO KNOW MORE ABOUT ME, MEET ME IN THE STALAGMITE CAVE.
DAN BAR-ON!

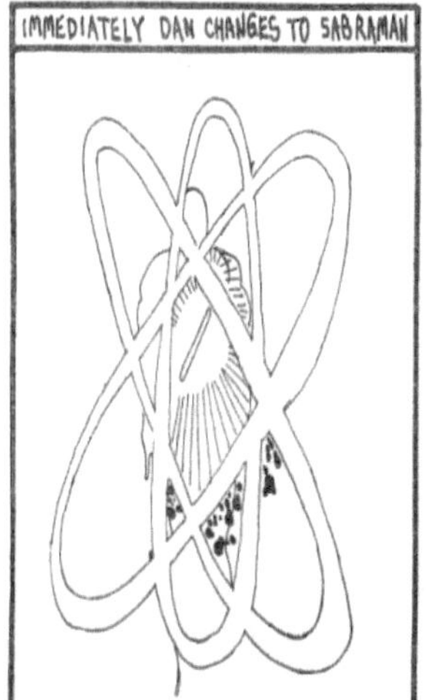
IMMEDIATELY DAN CHANGES TO SABRAMAN

SABRAMAN IS STILL WEAK FROM THE FIGHT WITH POWERMAN...

MOMENTS LATER HE IS OVER THE STALAGMITE CAVE...

OUT OF MY WAY!

SABRAMAN RUSHES INTO THE CAVE...

HIS EYES CAREFULLY PROBE ITS DARK RECESSES.

BUT HE DOESN'T SPOT THE DANGER OVERHEAD.
WELL, WHERE IS THE NEXT SURPRISE THAT HE PREPARED FOR ME ?

SUDDENLY...

ZOO

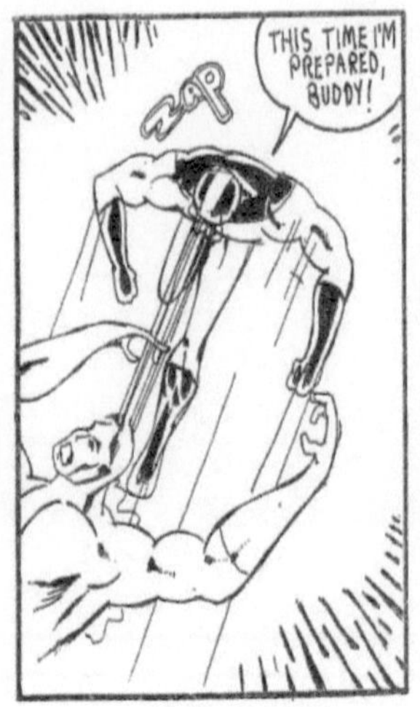
ZAP
THIS TIME I'M PREPARED, BUDDY!

BUT POWERMAN SHOVES SABRAMAN OVER.
HEY!!

POW
KRASH!

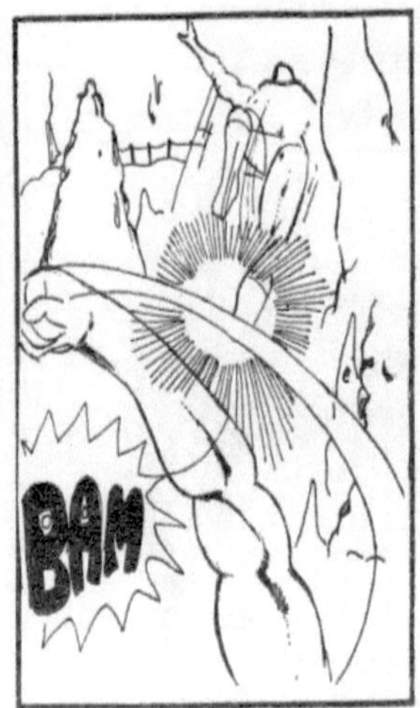
BAM

POW

I CAN SEE I'LL HAVE TO USE SOME OF MY SECRET POWERS TO FINISH THIS GUY...

HEY!
I'LL COLLECT ENERGY IN MY BODY BY NOT USING THE ATOMIC ROD FOR A WHILE... THERE!

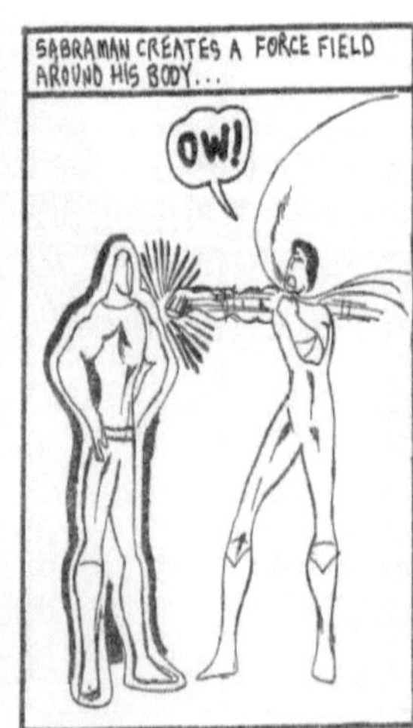
SABRAMAN CREATES A FORCE FIELD AROUND HIS BODY...
OW!

NOW I'LL CONCENTRATE ALL MY POWER IN MY HAND AND GIVE HIM A LITTLE RADIOACTIVE TOUCH.

ARGH!!

O.K. NOW, WISE GUY, YOU'RE PARALYZED FOR THE NEXT HOUR. NOW TALK! WHAT DO YOU WANT FROM ME ?
I DON'T TALK TO CREATURES LIKE YOU!
WHAT!?

ARE YOU CRAZY? I'M AN ISRAELI AGENT TRYING TO SAVE HUMANITY!
WHO'S YOUR BOSS ?
BUT MY BOSS TOLD ME YOU'RE TRYING TO BOMB THE WORLD!
STEVENS, CIA...

SABRAMAN SOARS INTO THE AIR...

CIA, HERE I COME !!

HE FLIES TOWARDS THE SEA . . .

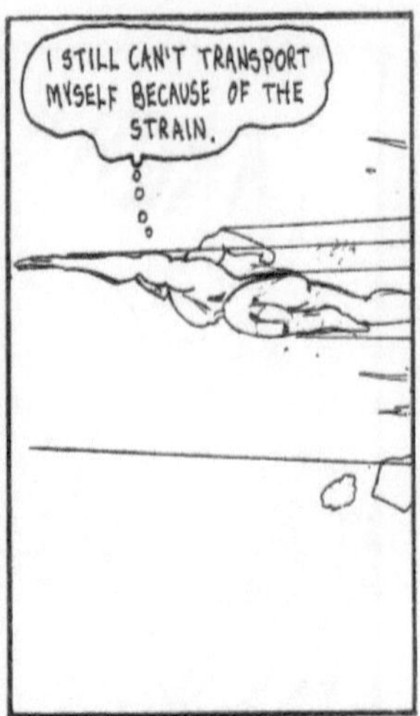
I STILL CAN'T TRANSPORT MYSELF BECAUSE OF THE STRAIN.

SABRAMAN APPROACHES THE SHORES OF THE UNITED STATES...

HERE I AM, U.S.A! THAT GUY STEVENS MUST BE SOMEWHERE IN THAT CIA BUILDING !

SABRAMAN SMASHES INTO STEVENS' OFFICE...
MERCIFUL HEAVENS !!!

BUT STEVENS MANAGES TO SOUND THE ALARM...
GUARDS! GUARDS! HELP!! SOMEONE'S TRYING TO KILL ME!

HE'S ESCAPING AND SENDING A ROBOT AFTER ME.

GOOD GRIEF! MY POWERS ARE GONE! PROBABLY BECAUSE OF THE STRAIN OF THE LONG FLIGHT FROM ISRAEL. THAT ROBOT IS SET ON KILL !!!

NOW I KNOW STEVENS IS GUILTY. WITH HIM I CAN OPEN AN INVESTIGATION, BUT THAT ROBOT . . . UGH... I'M LOSING CONSCIOUSNESS !!!

HEY! WHAT'S THIS!?
AN ELECTRIC WIRE! MAYBE IT WILL HELP ME.

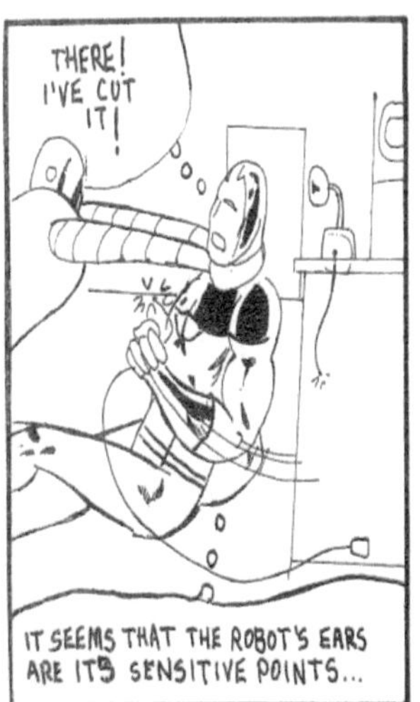
THERE! I'VE CUT IT!
IT SEEMS THAT THE ROBOT'S EARS ARE ITS SENSITIVE POINTS...

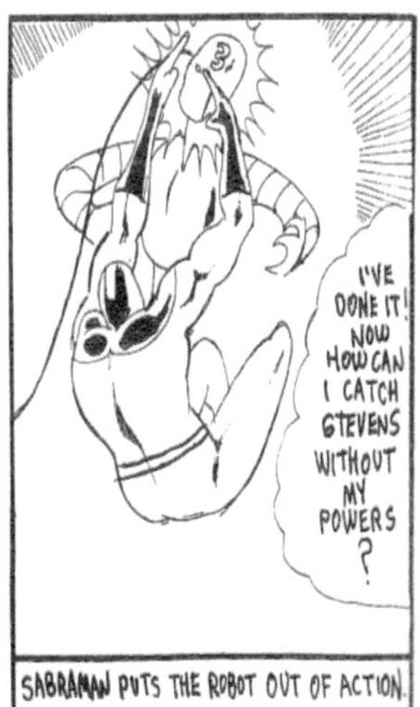
I'VE DONE IT! NOW HOW CAN I CATCH STEVENS WITHOUT MY POWERS?
SABRAMAN PUTS THE ROBOT OUT OF ACTION.

I'LL HAVE TO SWING ACROSS TOWN. HERE... THIS ROBOT'S WIRES WILL BE MY ROPES.

GULP!!

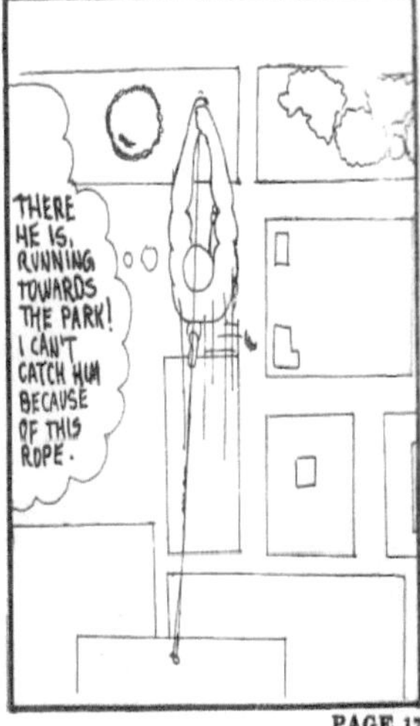
THERE HE IS, RUNNING TOWARDS THE PARK! I CAN'T CATCH HIM BECAUSE OF THIS ROPE.

WELL, MAYBE I CAN'T CATCH HIM, BUT I CAN DO...

...THIS!
POW

SPLASH

O.K. FELLAH! TALK!
HONEST, I DON'T KNOW ANYTHING! HE'S ALWAYS CALLING ON THE PHONE!

SOMETHING FALLS INTO THE WATER BEHIND STEVENS...
PLOP!
WELL, I THINK I CAN OPEN AN INVESTIGATION NOW...

AT THAT MOMENT STEVENS EXPLODES...

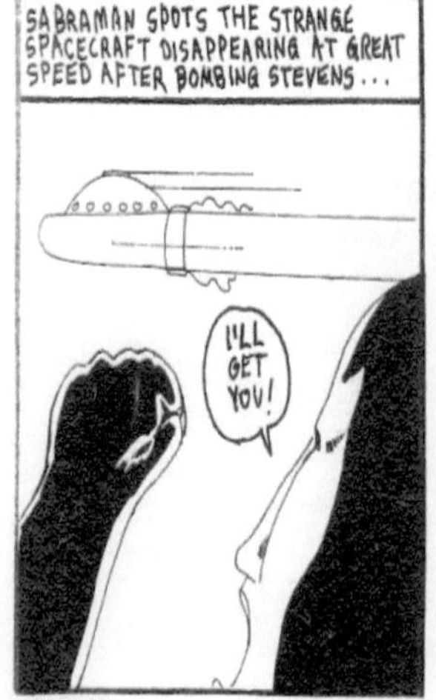
SABRAMAN SPOTS THE STRANGE SPACECRAFT DISAPPEARING AT GREAT SPEED AFTER BOMBING STEVENS...
I'LL GET YOU!

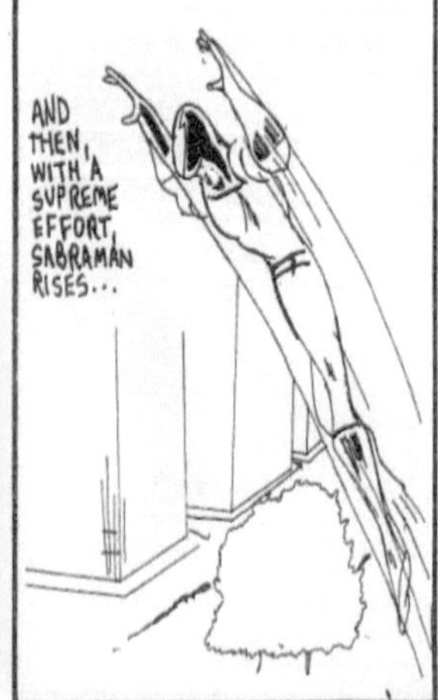
AND THEN, WITH A SUPREME EFFORT, SABRAMAN RISES...

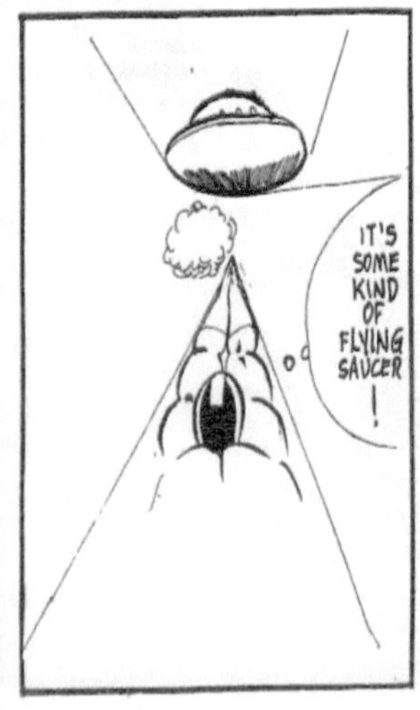
IT'S SOME KIND OF FLYING SAUCER!

SABRAMAN BURSTS INTO THE SAUCER...
KA-RASH!

WELCOME, MISTER ISRAELI STRONG MAN! NOW YOU'RE POWERLESS AGAIN! HA! HA! HA!

THE BOSS WILL GIVE ME AN EXTRA BONUS FOR FINISHING YOU TOO. AND ACCORDING TO CALCULATIONS YOU...

SHUT UP!
POW!
VIDEO

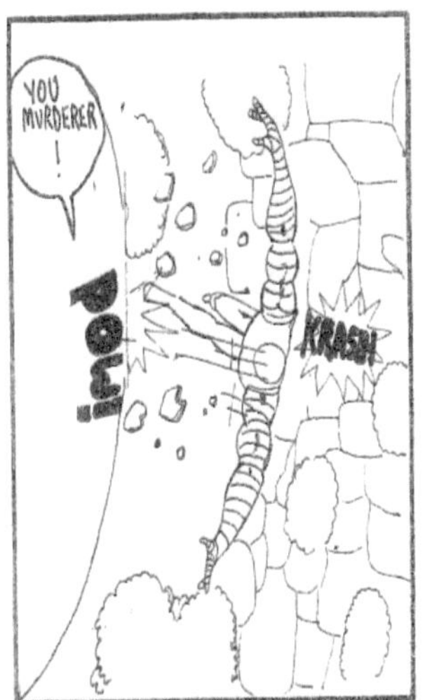
YOU MURDERER!
POW!
KRASH

I HOPE I CAN WORK THIS THING! IT'S VERY STRANGE... HE'S LETTING ME DRIVE IT...

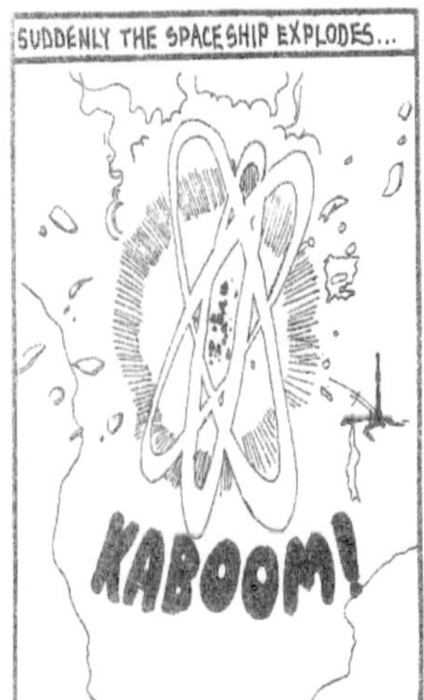
SUDDENLY THE SPACESHIP EXPLODES...
KABOOM!

THE FORCE OF THE EXPLOSION HURLS SABRAMAN CLEAR. UNCONSCIOUS, HE PLUMMETS DOWN TOWARDS A DESERT...

PLOOF!
A SAND-DUNE CUSHIONS THE IMPACT OF HIS FALL...

HE LIES THERE SILENTLY WHILE CONSCIOUSNESS GRADUALLY RETURNS...

UNTIL...
OH! OH! SOMEBODY IS BEHIND ME. PROBABLY ANOTHER TRAP!

NO, THIS CAN'T BE A TRAP. HE'S NOT SO STRONG AFTER ALL.
SURPRISE!

OOF
... BUT I'M STILL POWERLESS SO I'LL STILL HAVE TO DEFEND MYSELF

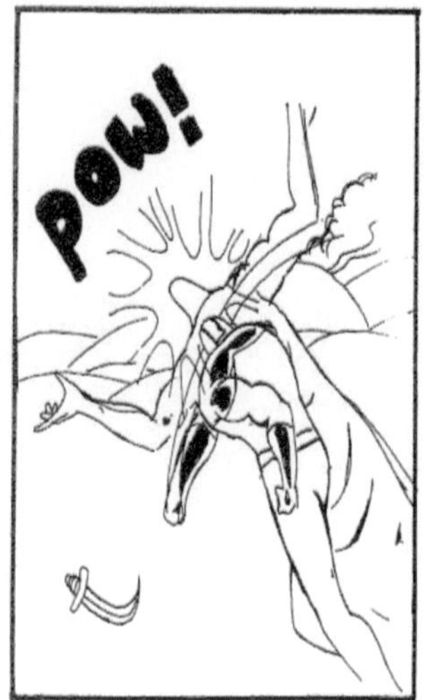
POW!

AFTER A BRIEF STRUGGLE SABRAMAN DOWNS HIS ADVERSARY ONLY TO FIND...

WHA...!?

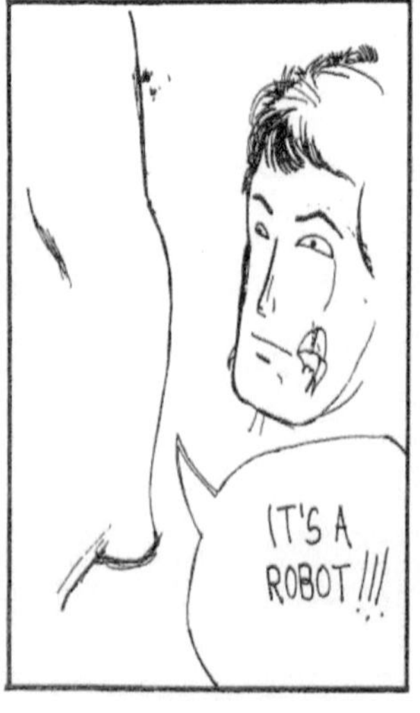
IT'S A ROBOT!!!

INSTINCTIVELY SABRAMAN FEELS SOMETHING IS WRONG. HE RUNS FOR HIS LIFE.
I'VE GOT TO GET OUT OF HERE !

SUDDENLY, A MIGHTY ATOMIC EXPLOSION.
BOOM

I FIGURED THAT IF THAT ROBOT WASN'T A STRONG ONE — AND MY MYSTERY MAN CAN SURE BUILD STRONG ONES — SO IT HAD TO BE ANOTHER SORT OF TRAP ... A BOMB! AN ATOMIC BOMB! IF I HAD BEEN IN THE EXPLOSION AREA I'D BE DONE FOR!
NOW I'LL TRY TO GET UP.

SOME HOURS LATER SABRAMAN COMES TO...
OH, THAT HURTS!! THE ROD IN MY WAS AFFECTED BY THE RADIATION BLAST.

BUT SABRAMAN LOSES CONSCIOUSNESS AGAIN
I'M NOT ... YMMH....

WHEN HE COMES TO, HE FINDS HIMSELF IN A VERY UNPLEASANT SITUATION...
?
GOOD DAY, DEAR FRIEND!

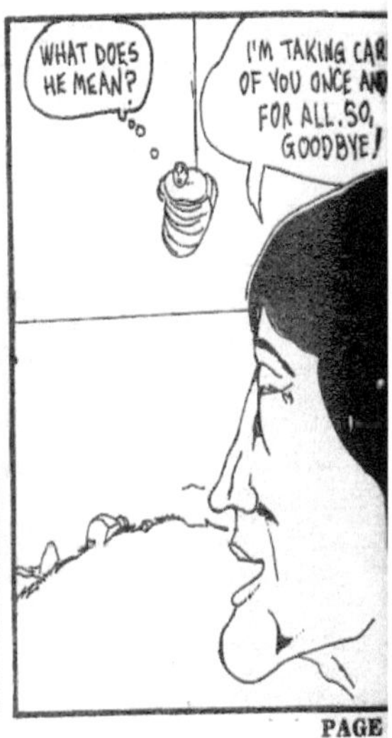
WHAT DOES HE MEAN?
I'M TAKING CAR OF YOU ONCE AND FOR ALL. SO, GOODBYE!

SNAP!
ZIP!

IN THE MURKY DEPTHS SABRAMAN RAPIDLY FREES HIMSELF...
HE MUST BE CRAZY, THINKING THAT A LITTLE WATER CAN FINISH ME!

GOOD GRIEF! A MONSTER!

UGH!!.. IT'S GRABBING ME!

HOW AM I GOING TO GET OUT OF THIS MESS?

HE'S GOING TO DEVOUR ME!

BUT IT TAKES MORE THAN A MONSTER TO FINISH SABRAMAN! HE BLASTS HIMSELF FREE!
THESE UNDER-WATER BLASTERS WORK JUST FINE!
ZAP!

HE HURTLES TOWARDS THE SURFACE...
WAIT A MOMENT, IT'S TOO EASY! IT'S NOT LIKE MY ENEMY TO BE SO CARE-LESS.

I'D BETTER CHECK BEFORE I SURFACE. I'LL THROW SOME ROCKS AND SEE WHAT HAPPENS.
JUST AS I SUSPECTED. AS SOON AS I SURFACE I GET ZAPPED!

THIS IS WHEN A TRANSPORTATION COMES IN HANDY!

LATER, BACK IN ISRAEL...
I'VE ALREADY REPORTED THIS CASE TO THE SUPERIORS SO WE CAN'T OPERATE NOW.
OH, COME ON BOSS.
SOMEONE'S TRYING TO KILL ME BECAUSE OF THOSE FILES. ISN'T THAT ENOUGH FOR AN INVESTIGATION !?

SABRAMAN LEAPS INTO ACTION...
GOODBYE, CHIEF !
HEY! WHERE ARE YOU GOING ?

ONCE AGAIN HE FLASHES ACROSS THE SKY OF ISRAEL.

HE ZOOMS DOWN ON THE SECRET BASE...

AHA! JUST AS I FIGURED!

SOMEONE'S STEALING THE FILES!

THE THIEF IS SOON OVERPOWERED...
OK. HE ADMITTED EVERYTHING. NOW YOU'VE GOT SOME EXPLAINING TO DO!

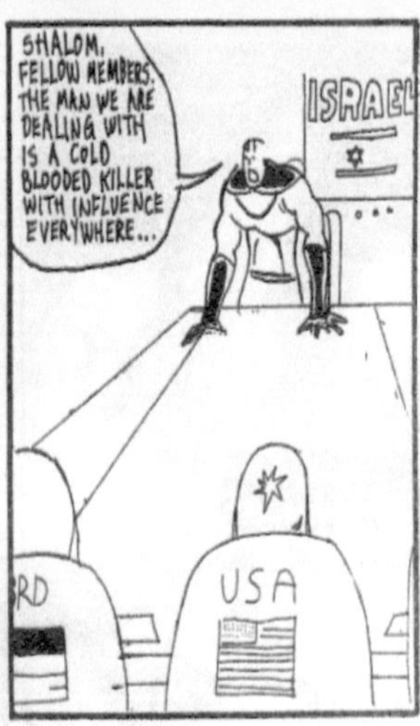

NEXT ISSUE: Can Sabraman defeat the Shadowman and save the world?

www.ingramcontent.com/pod-product-compliance
Ingram Content Group UK Ltd.
Pitfield, Milton Keynes, MK11 3LW, UK
UKHW041849190726
13854UKWH00002B/785

9 798776 063299